C000083096

Best Friends from Opposite Sides of the Tracks

Kenneth D. Brubaker Jr.

Best Friends from Opposite Sides of the Tracks

Kenneth D. Brubaker Jr.

ISBN: 978-1-63765-024-0
LCCN: 2021907632

Halo Publishing International, LLC
8000 W Interstate 10, Suite 600
San Antonio, Texas 78230
www.halopublishing.com

Printed and bound in the United States of America

This story and book are dedicated to my family. My two sons, Carson and Anderson, gave me the inspiration to write a book intended to educate children and their families. I am very thankful for my family in Buffalo, New York, the Brubaker family. They have always given me the support to pursue my passions and dreams.

Contents

About the Boys

Donny and Benny are from opposite sides of town. The town is called Sabreville. There are railroad tracks, which run straight through the middle of town. One side of the tracks is populated by people who are very wealthy. The other side consists of people who are not rich and are blue-collar, working-class families.

Robbery and other crimes happen often on Benny's side of town. Benny lives in the run-down, poor, and older side of town. Benny is biracial. His father is Black American, and his mom is white. He is an only child. He feels very fortunate to have a best friend like Donny.

Donny lives in the wealthy side of town. He and his family are very rich. He is also an only child. Donny and Benny spend almost every day together. Donny has awesome video and computer games. They always play them at his house. Donny also has a cool basement with a pool table, electronic dart board, and air hockey game. The two boys love to compete against each other. They also like basketball, always playing at Donny's house because he has a basketball hoop in his driveway.

The times that Benny does not see Donny are usually when Donny goes out of town with his parents to see his grandparents or to go on vacation.

Donny has many friends. He is usually the center of attention when others are around; he's quite popular in school and in his neighborhood. His mom is a stay-at-home mom, and his dad is a businessman. He travels for work and is not home much.

Although Donny is popular and rich, he treats everyone the same. He does not act as if he were better than everyone else. Benny really respects him for that.

Benny does not have many friends. He is often picked on at school. His parents are not rich. His mom is a part-time secretary and works from morning to afternoon. His dad works as a second- or third-shift factory worker. Benny very seldom sees his dad; he is usually asleep by the time his dad gets home. They manage, but times can be tough. Benny does not spend much time with his parents as a family.

When Donny goes over to Benny's house, which is not often, they play cards and talk about sports or what has been going on at school. Almost every time, during their card game, Benny's mom prepares snacks and sodas for them. In addition, on weekends, when Benny's dad is home, he will play cards with them.

Chapter 1

Class Presentations

Today at school, Donny and Benny's fourth-grade teacher, Mrs. Trimble, told the class that there were going to be class presentations that Friday. The presentations were to consist of stories regarding something special each child owned. That meant Benny only had a few days to come up with something good. In the past when it was show-and-tell day, Benny always had to scramble to find something to talk about.

After school, Benny went to Donny's house to play Mega Basketball on his computer. While they were playing, Donny said, "What are you bringing for the class presentation on Friday?"

Benny said, "I have no idea."

"I'm sure you will think of something. You usually come up with good things," said Donny.

After playing on the computer, the two boys went to Donny's basement to play air hockey. While they were doing that, Donny's mom came downstairs and said, "Benny, what are you going to take to your class presentation this time? Every year since kindergarten, Donny tells me about the things you bring for the show-and-tell project and the wonderful stories you tell about them."

Benny said, "I don't have anything yet."

Donny's mom tried to continue, but Donny interrupted and said, "It's not called show-and-tell anymore, Mom. They are called class presentations since we are now in fourth grade."

"Well, I remember when Donny told me about—"

Donny once again interrupted his mom and said, "Mom, can't you see we are playing an intense game here."

She then said, "Well, I'm sure it will be interesting."

They finished the air hockey game, and it was time for Benny to go home.

* * * * *

The next day after school, they played basketball in Donny's driveway. While they were shooting hoops, two of their good friends, Tommy and Petey, came to play basketball with them.

During the shootaround, Petey began to talk about the upcoming class presentations. He said, "I can't wait to show my new remote-control race car and talk about it for the class presentation!"

Then, Tommy said, "I can't wait to show my new train set!"

Donny changed the subject and said, "Let's play some ball."

* * * * *

The following day, Thursday, Tina, Heather, and Cindy, three girls who have a crush on Donny, came over to Donny and Benny while they were walking home from school. These girls were also from Donny's neighborhood and from rich families. The girls began to show off some of their nice jewelry and pretty necklaces that they were going to bring for the class presentations on Friday.

Tina jokingly said to Benny, "Benny, you probably will bring the diamond necklace from the Titanic that was lost at sea."

The girls laughed.

Benny did not respond.

However, Donny said, "You will see. Benny will have something good to show off and talk about."

Heather then said, "Sure he will."

Cindy chimed in and said, "Oh, I bet it will be amazing!"

The boys went on to Donny's house to shoot hoops and play basketball as the girls walked away laughing.

* * * * *

Well, the day Benny dreaded the most at school is here. Today is Friday, and it is the day everyone in the class has to stand up and talk about an item they brought to school. Everyone usually has something cool to show and talk about. Benny does not have much. In fact, Benny has absolutely nothing!

Now, before it is too late and the class presentations begin, he has to find something dazzling to show and talk about. Usually, Benny does not wait this long to find something, but, each time, it seems to be more and more difficult. In addition, once again, he will have to tell another great made-up story to the class to avoid feeling humiliated.

Benny does not know what to do or where to go to get something for the school presentation. He begins to panic. He is very nervous, his heart is pounding, and he is dreading what is going to happen. Benny has thought many times of telling his best friend, Donny, about this problem, but is too afraid of what he might think.

However, to Benny's surprise, just before the class presentations are to begin, Donny gives Benny an old, shiny gold pocket watch. He says, "Benny, my grandfather gave me this beautiful pocket watch. I want to give this to you. This is a very special pocket watch made out of gold. It is special to me because my grandfather wanted to give it to his one and only grandson. There is more to the story behind the pocket watch, but for now, take it and use it. I am sure you can come up with something great to tell the class."

Benny says, "Thank you, Donny. I'll come up with something great to say about it." Benny is very thankful Donny has given him something to show and talk about to their class.

Then, it hits Benny. Donny has known all along about his made-up show-and-tell stories. At first, Benny feels embarrassed. He does not know what to say to Donny. Then, Benny begins to ask him a question, "Hey, Donny, did you know about—"

Donny interrupts him and says, "I am sure you will do great." Donny smiles at Benny and then pats him on the shoulder. He gives him an "everything will be okay" look.

Benny no longer feels embarrassed. He is relieved because his best friend understands his feelings. Benny definitely appreciates Donny for understanding him and, most of all, for being his best friend.

Benny thinks long and hard about what to say about this pocket watch. As he rehearses the story in his head, he begins to feel awful. He asks himself, How can I lie about my best friend's pocket watch that was given to him by his grandfather? Benny continues to think long and hard.

As he is thinking, several boys from class walk by and start harassing him. One boy asks, "What crazy thing and story will you come up with this time for show-and-tell?"

Then, Benny notices it is only one minute before the class presentations are to start. He goes into class and sits down at his desk, trembling, heart pounding, nervous. Benny begins to write down some ideas, his heart still pounding and hand trembling. Kids in class are whispering and giggling around him. He can barely write.

All of a sudden, he hears the teacher, Mrs. Trimble, call out his name. "Benny, it is your turn to present. What great thing and story do you have to share with us this time?" she asks.

Benny stands up and goes to the front of the class. He just stands there for a few moments. Kids are giggling and whispering as Benny is standing there helpless, not sure what to do or say. Then, he begins to mumble—

Mrs. Trimble interrupts. "Speak louder; we can hardly hear you."

Kids laugh at Benny.

Then, a sudden warm and calm feeling comes over him, and he begins to talk louder and more clearly. "I just want to say thank you to my best friend, Donny. I have this beautiful pocket watch made of gold that he gave me to show and talk about. I was going to tell the class an amazing story about how I found this pocket watch, but I would have been lying, just like all the other times I have lied."

Some of the kids in class continue to giggle, while others look surprised.

"I have decided to talk about my best friend instead. Donny is my best friend; I enjoy spending time with him. Today, I found out that he truly understands me, and did even during the past times when I lied. I want to thank Donny for giving me his grandfather's pocket watch. I am certain Donny's grandfather gave him this pocket watch because he feels that Donny is someone special. I know this because Donny does look out for me, and everyone else, for that matter. So, for me, this pocket watch is a symbol of our friendship and a symbol of truth."

Some of the kids in class applaud while others are still giggling and whispering to each other.

Still, Benny feels at peace with himself. When he goes to sit down, he looks at Donny and knows he is surprised because of the look on his face. Donny is red in the face, somewhat embarrassed. After a few moments, the two best friends look at each other again, and Donny nods at Benny with approval.

When Benny gives the pocket watch back, Donny leans over to him and says, "That was a pretty cool thing you said up there." Then, he gives Benny a fist bump.

Chapter II

Donny and Benny Find a New Best Friend

One beautiful spring day after school, Donny and Benny took a walk down the railroad tracks to sit by Sabre Lake. They usually sat on a bank under the bridge, where the train passed over. That was the spot they went to get away from town, enjoy the beautiful scenery of the lake, and just talk.

While they were talking about the upcoming summer basketball season, Benny noticed something coming towards them from a distance. It was moving along the side of the lake. Benny said, "Donny, look, there is a dog by the lake!"

Both boys began to run to see what the dog was doing. As they approached the dog, they noticed it was limping. Donny went ahead of Benny, knelt down a distance away from the dog so as not to startle it. Donny said in a soft voice, "Come here, boy, come here."

The dog began to turn and go the other way. As it was limping down the lakeside, it would stop and take a drink of water.

Benny said, "What should we do? He is afraid of us."

Donny glanced at Benny with a puzzled look. Then, he said, "Benny, wait here. I am going to try something."

"Okay," Benny replied with a sigh.

With a limp, Donny began to walk towards the dog, trying to show the dog that he was injured too.

Benny just stood and watched, wondering what his best friend was doing.

To get the dog's attention, Donny fell to the ground and whimpered as if he were in pain.

The dog sat down and just looked at Donny. Then, the dog began to limp and inch towards Donny, as if it wanted to help him.

Donny just lay still and kept whimpering.

Then, when the dog finally got to Donny, it laid its head down on Donny's chest.

Donny slowly began to pet the dog and said, "It will be okay, boy. Everything will be okay." Donny then motioned Benny to come over.

As Benny was walking towards the wounded dog and Donny, he overheard Donny saying, "It's okay, boy. Benny is here to help." Donny nodded at Benny and said, "Go ahead; pet him."

Benny looked at Donny, smiled, and began to softly pet the dog.

As Donny was picking the dog up to carry it, he said to Benny, "We need to get his leg looked at."

Benny said, "I wonder what happened to him. He looks pretty dirty and beat up."

Donny agreed and said, "Let's take him to the vet in town and see if they can help him."

Once the boys got the dog to the veterinarian's office, a vet quickly took the dog from Donny's arms. When the vet did that, the dog began to whimper. The whimper got louder and louder as they disappeared into one of the rooms.

The vet, who seemed quite concerned, returned and said, "Well, it looks like we will need you two boys in here with us."

The two boys quickly went to be with the dog.

The veterinarian introduced herself saying, "I am Doctor Holmes, but you can call me Mary."

As Mary was looking over the dog, she asked the boys several questions about how the dog was hurt. Of course, the boys had no idea how; their main concern was what was going to happen to the dog now.

As Mary was cleaning the dog and bandaging its leg, she asked, "So, who is the owner?"

The boys looked at each other, and Benny said, "We don't know. We found the dog near the lake."

Mary said, "This dog has really hurt its leg." Then, she asked, "Does the dog have a collar?"

Donny said, "No, it didn't have a collar when we found it."

"Hmmm, I guess we will keep the dog here and post some flyers to find out if there is an owner," said Mary.

Then, Donny spoke up, "We will take care of it."

Mary said, "If no one claims the dog after a couple of weeks, I will see what we can do. Until then, if you would like to visit the dog, you are welcome to."

Benny and Donny looked at Mary with concern. Then, they went over to the dog, petted it, and began to walk away.

As they were leaving, the dog began to whimper once again.

Donny and Benny looked back, with saddened looks on their faces, before walking toward the door.

Benny said to the vet, "Mary, if somebody does claim the dog, can we meet that person?"

Donny then said, "Yeah, we need to meet this person."

Mary said, "Don't worry. I will let you know and try to make that happen."

Donny walked over to the dog once more, hugged it, and then whispered in his ear, "Don't worry, buddy. We will be back for you."

As the two boys walked out, the dog continued to whimper.

* * * * *

The next day after school, Donny and Benny went to visit the dog.

The vet, Mary, met them in her office and said, "The dog is resting. Would you like to see him?"

Of course, the boys were excited to see him. They followed Mary to where the dog was resting. When the boys got to the dog's cage, the dog pushed his nose and mouth through it as if to give the boys kisses.

Donny asked Mary, "Can we take him out of the cage?"

Mary said, "Okay, but you need to hold him. I do not want to have him on that hurt leg just yet." Mary took the dog out of the cage and handed it to Donny.

As Donny was holding him, the dog just wanted to give him kisses. When Donny gave the dog to Benny, the same thing happened; the dog wanted to kiss Benny.

Mary said, "Boys, this dog has been whimpering all day until now."

Donny sprang up and said, "We really want to take care of the dog."

Mary replied, "Well, I am not going to let you take him home just yet, but you can help me take care of him."

Benny said, "How can we help?"

Mary answered, "Come by every day, nurture him, and help take care of him. You both can do that by feeding him food and giving him water. And, of course, pet him and show him you care for him. Then, this weekend, we will try to get him up on his leg to do some exercises."

Donny and Benny were pleased.

Benny said, "Okay, we can do that."

Both boys smiled, petted, and hugged the dog one last time before they left.

* * * * *

The next day after school, the boys decided to play cards and talk about a possible new name for the dog before they went to the vet's office. During one of their poker hands, Benny showed he had an ace-high, which won the hand.

As the boys were talking about names, Benny kept mumbling to himself. "Ace—that's it!" he said loudly. "Ace, we can call him Ace!"

Donny replied, "Yeah, Ace because he is one of a kind."

The two boys agreed and were happy with the name.

When the boys arrived at the vet's office, they decided that they were going to try to get the dog used to his new name. They told Mary about the new name.

She said, "Boys, he cannot use that name yet. He may have a name already."

Donny looked at Benny and said, "That's true. We need to wait before giving him a name."

Mary then said, "If no one claims the dog by next Friday, I will let you take him home. Now, tomorrow, make sure you stop by so we can try to get the dog up on its feet."

Donny and Benny then walked to where the dog was in his cage. Benny picked him up, and as usual, the dog perked up and began to give kisses to both boys.

* * * * *

It was finally the weekend. Saturday morning, after breakfast and a card game, Donny and Benny went to the vet's office. They were excited to help the dog with its exercises.

Once they arrived, they joined Mary in the playroom of the vet's office. Mary was trying to get the dog to stand up.

Nothing happened. The dog just lay on the ground and whimpered.

Mary then turned to the two boys and said, "Okay, which one of you wants to give this a try?"

Of course, both boys wanted to try first.

"Hmmm. Let's try this," said Mary. "Donny, you help hold the dog so his feet are on the ground, and, Benny, you take a dog biscuit and call the dog over to you."

Benny ran to get a dog biscuit off the counter, returned, held it out to the dog, and started by saying, "C'mon, boy, come on; you can do it."

As Benny held the biscuit out in front of the dog, the dog began to move away from Donny. As it moved towards Benny, it was limping.

Donny went to help, but Mary said, "Donny, it's okay. He needs to try on his own."

Donny looked worried. Watching the dog struggle to get the biscuit, his heart dropped to his stomach.

Finally, after several minutes, the dog made it over to Benny and began to eat the biscuit.

Benny and Donny cheered for the dog and gave it a hug.

Mary said, "Okay, Donny, you take a turn, and then we will call it a day."

The same result happened. The dog made it over to Donny and ate another biscuit.

The boys then took the dog to the cage and gave it one last hug before they left.

As the days went by, the boys were making progress with the wounded dog. The dog was now running through mazes and tunnels and was chasing tennis balls in the playroom.

* * * * *

It was finally Friday. After school, Benny and Donny started out for the vet's office. As they were walking to get their new dog, Donny said, "Benny, this is the day. This is the day we bring home our new dog."

Benny asked, "Donny, whose house will it stay at?"

"Hmm, I didn't even think of that," Donny replied.

Benny said, "I have told my parents about the dog and how we are helping him, but I haven't asked if I could keep him."

Donny said, "Well, I have told my parents about the dog too, but I haven't asked if I could keep him either."

Benny then raised his voice and said, "I know! Let's build a doghouse for him."

"But, whose house and yard will we keep him at?" asked Donny.

"Umm, well, who will stay with him when we are at school?" asked Benny.

Donny replied, "My mom is home all day; maybe she will look after the dog."

"Are you sure?" Benny asked.

"Yeah, we can build the doghouse and put it in my backyard. And, hopefully, my mom will look after the dog."

When they got to the vet's office, Mary was busy talking with someone. It was an old man with a cane. As they were talking, Mary kept looking in the direction of Benny and Donny.

Donny walked over to her and asked, "Mary, may I use the phone?"

"Sure, but use the phone in my office. Follow me," she said. Mary showed him the way and then said, "Here, use my office phone. I need to talk to the gentleman at the front desk."

Donny called his house. "Hi, Mom!" Donny began excitedly. "Umm, I was wondering if we can keep the dog that me and Benny found. You know, the dog that we have been taking care of at the vet's?"

Donny's mom asked, "So, the owner hasn't come to pick the dog up yet?"

"No," replied Donny, "and today is Friday, the day the vet said, if no one claims the dog, then we get it!"

"Well, as long as you take care of it when you get home from school and on weekends," Donny's mom replied.

Donny enthusiastically said, "Oh yes, indeed, me and Benny will definitely take care of it! Thanks, Mom!"

She then said, "I will let your dad know. I'm sure he'll be okay with it since he grew up with dogs in his house when he was your age."

"Love ya, Mom, and I'll see you later," said Donny.

Meanwhile, as Donny was talking on the phone with his mom, Benny overheard the conversation between Mary and the old man. Benny overheard the old man asking about his dog. He also heard Mary say that he was healing, and that he would be okay.

Donny then ran out of Mary's office, all excited to tell Benny the good news. "Benny! Benny! My mom said it is okay for the dog to stay at my house!"

However, Benny did not look happy at all. He looked as if someone had just hit him in the stomach.

"What's wrong, Benny?" asked Donny.

Just then, Mary walked over to the boys and said, "Boys, I would like you to meet the owner of the dog that you found. This is Mr. Holiday."

Shocked, Donny looked at her. He could not speak. The only things the boys could do were just stand and look at the old man.

The old man approached the two boys and said, "Thank you for takin' care of my dog. He means a great deal to me."

Benny and Donny still just looked at him, unable to talk.

Mary then said, "C'mon, boys, let's take Mr. Holiday to his dog."

Mr. Holiday said, "I am really glad that Skipper is okay."

When they got to Skipper's cage, the dog began to get excited and bark repeatedly.

After Mary got the dog out of the cage, the old man took him and held him. As he was holding the dog, the dog kept looking at the boys and barking loudly. Mr. Holiday said, "Oh, I see. You are excited to see the two boys who took care of you."

The boys got closer to the dog, and the dog leaned toward them and began to give kisses to both boys.

"Hmm, I think you have found new friends, haven't you?" said Mr. Holiday.

Mary interrupted and said to Benny and Donny, "Mr. Holiday and I were talking, and he said he would like it if you two boys could take care of Skipper."

Confused, the boys looked at each other. "What do you mean?" asked Donny.

Mr. Holiday said, "I want you boys to take care of Skipper. He needs to be able to do the things that dogs like to do. I am eighty-five years old now. See, I am too old to take care of Skipper. He needs a new family. And from what Mary has told me about you two boys, well, who better to take care of Skipper and provide him a new home?"

Benny and Donny looked at each other again, and then both yelled, "Wooo-hoooo!! All right!" They high-fived each other, hugged, and then gave Skipper hugs and kisses.

Benny said to the old man, "We thought you were going to take him away."

Donny asked, "Do you know how Skipper was hurt?"

Mr. Holiday said, "Yep. Skipper likes to jump, and he jumped right out of the living room window, which I had left open. See, I cannot get around very well, and before I could go after Skipper, he was out of sight. I think Skipper wants a new life, and, by golly, I am willing to give him that."

Benny said, "We were going to name him Ace if no one claimed him."

Donny then said, "Benny, I think Skipper is a great name."

Benny agreed and said, "Skipper it is. I like it too."

The two boys walked over to Mr. Holiday and shook his hand.

Mr. Holiday then said, "If you boys don't mind, I would like for you and Skipper to visit me once in a while."

The boys smiled and said, "Absolutely, Mr. Holiday."

Mr. Holiday gave Skipper one last hug before he left.

Mary then said to the boys, "Well, boys, I have some papers for you to show your parents and have them sign. Skipper will need to have a checkup once every few months. You will also need to hold on to his medical records."

The boys replied happily, "We will, Mary; we will."

After all the paperwork was done, sorted out, and given to the two boys, Benny and Donny walked their new dog to its new home.

Chapter III

Coping with Peer Pressure

Summer is approaching, and it is almost time for the Sabreville Basketball League to start. Tryouts are in a week. Benny and Donny love to play basketball. They play one-on-one or pickup games at either Sabreville Park or Donny's house, on his half-sized basketball court located in his driveway, towards the back of his house. Benny and Donny sometimes play with their friends Lamont, Leon, Tommy, Petey, and the two brothers, Carson and Anderson. They make up teams and play a four-on-four pickup game.

Those children who try out for the Summer Sabreville Basketball League are assigned to a team. However, the team to play for is the Knights. It's usually the best team in the league every year. Hometown hero, Mr. Jordan, coaches the team.

* * * * *

One day after school, while the boys were playing a four-on-four pickup basketball game at Sabreville Park, four boys from their school approached them. The boys' names were Kyle, Tony, Jake, and Jimmy. These four boys, just like Donny, had very rich families; they were jocks and, of course, very popular in school. The four boys walked up to Donny and began to talk quietly.

Kyle said, "Hey, Donny, you and Tommy are pretty good basketball players. Why don't you and Tommy play on our team for the Sabreville summer league?"

Donny hesitated and then asked, "How do you know what team you will be on?"

Kyle laughed and said, "Me, you, Tony, Jake, Jimmy, and Tommy are the best players in the league. Usually, the best players in the league play for the Knights and Coach Jordan."

Tony said, "So, what do you say?"

Donny said, "It would be great to play on your team, but I hope to play on a team with my other friends."

The four boys laughed, and Jake said, "There is no chance of that happening."

Then, Benny came over and asked, "Would you guys like to play the winners of our game?"

The four boys laughed again, and Jimmy said, "No thanks."

Kyle then said, "Why are you not a good basketball player, Benny? I mean, by your looks, you should be better."

Benny, being biracial and of color, knew what Kyle meant. He was speechless.

Then, the two brothers, Carson and Anderson, came over to the group of boys and said, "What's going on?"

Benny, embarrassed and humiliated, did not say a word.

Donny, trying to end the conversation, said, "Let's play some ball."

Anderson and Carson asked the other four boys again, "Are you going to play the winners of this game?"

Kyle said, "We don't want to humiliate and embarrass you guys."

Then, Tony said, "We will see you at tryouts on Saturday."

As the four boys were walking away after making fun of Benny, Donny, and their friends, Jake said jokingly, "We are going to get some girls for you to play against and watch you lose." All four of them laughed.

Benny and Donny did not say much as they rode their bikes home from Sabreville Park. When they arrived at the Sabreville railroad tracks, Benny said to Donny, "I hope we are on the same team this summer."

Donny responded, "I don't know what will happen after tryouts. I would like to play ball with all of my friends."

Benny replied, "Me too."

Donny said, "I'm tired. I'll see you tomorrow."

Benny said, "See ya tomorrow."

The boys then rode their bikes in opposite directions to go home.

* * * * *

The next day at school, while Donny was at his locker, Kyle, Tony, Jake, and Jimmy walked over to him, and Tony said, "Donny, we have a pretty good idea of who is going to play for the Knights."

Donny asked, "How do you know who is playing for the Knights? We haven't had tryouts yet."

Kyle stepped closer to Donny and said, "Donny, every year the best players in Sabreville are put together on the same team, the Knights! They put the best players on the same team because, if the league keeps the best players together, then in junior high and high school, we give our school a better chance of winning every year."

Jake said, "So, what do you say, Donny?"

Before Donny could respond, Jimmy said, "Yeah, Donny, what do you say?"

Donny, trying to think of what to say, just blurted out, "Okay!"

The four boys smiled; then, Kyle patted Donny on the shoulder and said, "Let's go win a championship."

Tony then came nearer, put his arm around Donny, and said, "Yeah, you don't want to be humiliated with your other so-called friends."

Donny, still not knowing what to say, gave a nervous smile, nodded his head, and walked away.

* * * * *

After school, Donny and Benny rode their bikes to Donny's house to finish building Skipper's doghouse. Every day after school, Skipper would be at the backyard fence, waiting for the two boys. As Skipper saw them, he would jump up high and bark loudly, excited to play with the boys. Always, when they got up to the backyard fence, Skipper acted as if he were trying to jump over the fence to greet the boys.

While the boys were working on the doghouse, their friend Petey stopped over. He said to Donny and Benny with excitement, "Hey, guys, guess what? My dad is going to coach a team for the summer basketball league! My dad said he will try to get me, the both of you, Tommy, Lamont, Leon, Carson, and Anderson to play on the team he is going to coach. We are going to be called the Gladiators!"

Benny smiled, looked at Donny, and put his hand up, as if to give Donny a high five.

Donny looked at Benny, then turned to Petey, and said, "How do we know for sure we will be on the same team? What if one of us is chosen to play for another team?"

Petey said, "My dad says that the coaches usually talk after tryouts and try to decide how teams should be made up."

Donny then said, "I heard that the best players are put on Coach Jordan's team, the Knights."

Petey responded, "I really don't know about that."

Benny then said, "All we can do is hope we are all on the same team."

Donny changed the subject and said, "Okay, Benny, let's finish Skipper's doghouse."

After Petey left, Benny and Donny continued building Skipper's doghouse. While they were working on it, Benny said, "Donny, I bet you get picked to play for the Knights. You are one of the best basketball players in town."

Donny said, "Thanks, Benny."

As the afternoon progressed, they did not say much more to each other. It was obvious both boys were still worried about tryouts on Saturday and which team they were going to be chosen to be a part of.

Benny, feeling the uncomfortable silence, said, "Donny, do you really want to play with Kyle and his friends?"

Donny replied, "Benny, they are my friends too—"

Benny interrupted Donny and said, "But you heard what Kyle said when we asked him if they wanted to play the next game… They said they didn't want to embarrass us or humiliate us."

Donny responded, "Benny, you are right. They should not have said that. But I can't help it if I am chosen to play with those guys and the Knights."

Benny gave Donny a concerned look and then smiled and said, "Let's finish Skipper's doghouse and see if he likes it."

Donny agreed and the boys continued to work on and finish the doghouse. By then, it was late.

Benny and Donny placed Skipper in the doghouse to see if he would like it. Skipper walked in and out of it, played with his dog toys for a while, and then lay down inside to fall asleep. The boys agreed that Skipper would enjoy his new doghouse.

Before Benny left, he said to Donny, "Donny, how about after school tomorrow we take Skipper with us and go visit Mr. Holiday?"

Donny replied, "Yeah, I think we should do that. Skipper probably misses Mr. Holiday."

Benny then said, "Sounds like a plan. See ya tomorrow."

Donny said, "See you tomorrow, Benny."

Benny got on his bike and rode home to the opposite side of town.

* * * * *

At school the next day at lunch, Donny and Benny were sitting with their good friends Tommy, Petey, Lamont, Leon, Carson, and Anderson. And, of course, sitting at the next table over were

Tina, Heather, and Cindy, all staring at Donny. Donny, the character that he can be, always gave them a wink and a wave. The three girls would then giggle and continue to talk about whatever girls talk about.

While eating lunch, Kyle came over with Tony and said sarcastically, "Donny, why do you always sit here with these guys during lunchtime? Why don't you sit with the guys from your neighborhood?"

Before Donny could respond, Kyle and Tony started to walk away. As they were doing so, Kyle said, "Tommy, why don't you come over here and sit with us?"

Now, Tommy, Petey, Lamont, Leon, Carson, and Anderson lived on the same side of town as Benny, that being the opposite side of town from Kyle and his friends. And for some reason, cliques had formed between these two sides of town.

Tommy looked at Kyle with uncertainty and then back towards his friends. Tommy was a very quiet boy and did not say much. He usually went along with what everyone else in the group was doing. But, surprising his friends, Tommy slowly stood up, grabbed his lunch tray, and walked over to the table at which Kyle and his friends were going to sit.

Donny and Benny, with stunned looks on their faces, stared at each other in shock. Everyone at the table became completely silent. For a few moments, no one said a word.

Then, Benny, with a disappointed look on his face, said, "What is Tommy doing? Those aren't his friends—"

Donny interrupted Benny and said, "Think about it, Benny. Tommy may not be a popular boy in school, but he is a really good basketball player."

Benny responded, "But that's not right. We are his friends, not them. We need to talk with him. Donny, those are your friends too; go find out what is going on."

Donny then said, "Benny, as I said before, they want him to play basketball on their summer-league team—"

Before Donny could finish what he was saying, Benny interrupted and said, "Well, someone needs to go tell Tommy that."

Donny responded, "Tommy will probably figure that out for himself; don't worry."

For the rest of the lunch period, the boys sat quietly, not saying much as they watched their good friend Tommy sitting and talking with his supposedly new friends.

* * * * *

After school, just as Donny and Benny had planned, they picked up Skipper and took him over to the middle of town to see his former owner, Mr. Holiday. When the boys and Skipper got to Mr. Holiday's house, Mr. Holiday was sitting outside in his rocking chair on the front porch.

When Skipper saw Mr. Holiday, Skipper ran up to his former owner, jumped on his lap, and began to give him kisses.

55

Mr. Holiday said, "Hi, boys, I didn't know you were coming over today. You usually bring Skipper to see me on the weekends."

Benny said, "We wanted to surprise you and bring Skipper over today."

Mr. Holiday replied, "Well, thanks, I do love seeing Skipper." He then asked, "Would you boys like some lemonade?"

Of course, the boys said yes and sat down on the porch with Skipper and Mr. Holiday. While they were talking about how Skipper liked his new doghouse, Benny decided to change the subject.

He asked Mr. Holiday, "How would you feel if one of your friends found new friends and started hanging out more with them than his closer friends?"

Mr. Holiday sat for a few moments, thinking, and said, "Well, Benny, Skipper found new friends. And he seems pretty happy with his new friends."

Benny and Donny looked at each other and then back at Mr. Holiday with a look of understanding.

As the boys were talking to Mr. Holiday, Skipper was lying peacefully on Mr. Holiday's lap. The boys really enjoyed listening to Mr. Holiday's stories. Especially stories of when he was in the navy and the experiences he had.

After a few hours of talking with Mr. Holiday, Donny and Benny walked over to him. They both shook his hand, thanked him for the lemonade, picked Skipper up off his lap, and said good-bye.

* * * * *

It was Saturday, the first day of summer-league basketball, the day for tryouts at Sabreville Elementary School. The boys from opposing sides of town, of course, were shooting on opposite sides of the court to warm up. At one point during the warm-up, Donny and Benny met at half-court, gave each other a high five, and wished each other luck.

Before they went to opposite sides of the court again, Benny asked Donny, "Have you talked with Tommy yet?"

Donny responded quickly, "No, not yet."

Benny was about to say something, but Donny quickly gave him another high five and ran to the opposite side of the court.

Once the warm-up concluded, the coaches started to have the players begin their tryouts. When the last drill was over, the coaches were called out into the hallway of the school to choose teams. Tension was high, and you could tell the boys seemed stressed about which team they would play for.

As Benny and Donny stood there looking at each other, very nervous, Coach Jordan walked back into the gym and began to call out the names of the players for his team. He shouted, "Kyle, Jake, Jimmy, Tony." He then paused.

Donny dropped his head down, and Benny was just not able to stand still. They could not take the suspense any longer.

Then, Coach Jordan continued, "Tommy and Donny."

As soon as Benny heard the last two names, he stood frozen, unable to move.

As expected, the best players, the players from the wealthy part of town, were chosen to play for Coach Jordan and the Knights.

Donny could barely walk over to the Knights' side of the gym.

As he did, Benny still stood there shocked and disappointed.

The worse players, the players from the blue-collar, poor part of town, were going to play for Mr. Olander, Petey's father. Petey's father, coach of the Gladiators, started to call out the names of the players that would play for him. He called out, "Benny, Lamont, Leon, Petey, Carson, and Anderson."

He continued to call out two more players, but Benny just stood there, not moving, in the middle of the gym. As he looked over at the Knights' side of the gym, he noticed several of the boys gesturing a thumbs-down and smiling, laughing at Benny as he remained in place, still shocked and unable to move to the Gladiators' side of the gym.

Donny just stayed where he was, head down, on the Knights' side, unable to look at Benny. Once Benny finally realized he really was not going to be on his best friend's team, he put his own head down in disappointment and walked to his side of the gym.

* * * * *

The league is separated into two divisions, the East and West Divisions. The Knights, Bobcats, Broncos, and Warriors play in the West Division; the Gladiators, Spartans, Wolverines, and Bulls in the East Division. Each team plays every other twice; however, they only play teams within their division. Every team is seeded and automatically makes the play-offs.

* * * * *

As time passed by, Donny finally mustered up the courage, walked over to Benny, and asked, "Benny, listen, no hard feelings, right?"

Benny peered at Donny and said, "You knew you were going to be picked to play for the Knights, didn't you?"

Donny looked at Benny with a sad face. Donny started to talk—

But Benny interrupted him before he could say one word. Benny said sarcastically, "You and Tommy have fun playing for the Knights." Benny then walked away from his best friend.

The next week at school, which was the last week before summer vacation, Donny and Benny did not talk to each other. Finally, on the last day of school, during lunch, Donny walked over to Benny and his usual group of friends and asked, "Can I sit here and talk with you guys?"

Everyone at the lunch table looked at each other for a few moments without saying anything. Then, Petey said, "Sure, Donny."

Donny sat next to Petey and across from his best friend, Benny. Donny said to Benny, "Hey, listen, I cannot help what team I am chosen to play for. I have to play for the team that chooses me."

Benny did not look at Donny while Donny was talking. He just sat there and did not say a word. The tension at the table was beginning to become unbearable.

Then, the two brothers, Carson and Anderson, who were considered the class clowns or funny ones of the group and school, stood up, placed whoopee cushions on their seats, and sat down.

After the awful noise of the whoopee cushions, everyone in the cafeteria began to laugh. Donny and Benny looked at each other and also laughed.

Carson said, "Who tooted?"

Anderson responded, "Oops, I think that was me."

The group at the table laughed even louder now. The tension among the group was definitely broken. The subject of conversation was changed, and the boys decided to talk about things other than summer-league basketball.

Chapter IV

The Unexpected

School is out and summer vacation has begun. Summer basketball is now in full swing. As expected, the Knights are in first place in the West Division. As for Benny and the Gladiators, they are in third place, and improving, in the East Division.

It is a Saturday afternoon, and Benny's team just won their game.

* * * * *

Benny decided to go to Donny's house to see if he wanted play. Benny rang the doorbell.

Donny came to the door and said, "Hey, Benny, what's up?"

Donny looked upset or just not himself. Benny could tell something was wrong. Benny asked, "Do you want to come out and play with Skipper or something?"

Donny said, "Nah, I really don't feel like it. But you can take Skipper out and play with him in the yard."

Benny said, "Okay, I will."

Both boys then paused and looked at each other as if they wanted to say something.

After the pause, Donny said quietly and sadly, "See ya later, Benny." Before Benny could reply, Donny closed the door.

* * * * *

Benny proceeded to get Skipper and take him for a walk. As Benny was doing so, he decided to go visit Mr. Holiday.

Once again, Mr. Holiday provided a glass of lemonade, and he and Benny talked awhile. Mr.

Holiday could tell there was something wrong. He asked Benny, "Benny, what is wrong? You do not seem like yourself today."

Benny said, "I think me and Donny are growing apart as friends, and I do not know why."

Mr. Holiday asked, "Well, why don't you talk with Donny?"

Benny said, "It's just awkward between us. Not playing on the same basketball team just doesn't seem right, and it is affecting our friendship."

Mr. Holiday said, "Talk with him, Benny. Until you truly know what is going on, it will continue to bother you."

Benny nodded and said, "Yeah, I guess you are right. I will try my best to talk with him." Benny stood up, shook hands with Mr. Holiday, wished him well, and walked Skipper home.

* * * * *

The regular season of the Sabreville Basketball League is over. It's time for the play-offs to begin. The Knights are undefeated and in first place in their division. The Gladiators are still in third place in their division, but the good thing about this league is that all teams make the play-offs.

Donny and Benny are still not talking much. Basketball practice has taken up a lot of their time, and every time Benny tries to call Donny, Donny is busy at home or out doing something.

Finally, it is the first day of play-offs. Benny's team wins a close game against the second-place team, the Spartans, and advances. Of course, he hears that Donny's team, the Knights, crushed their opponent, the Bobcats.

* * * * *

After the game, Benny decided to ride over to Donny's house to talk. When he got there, Donny's mom greeted him.

She said, "Go on upstairs. Donny is in his room."

Benny knocked on Donny's door.

Donny opened it and said quietly, "Hey, Benny."

Right away, Benny could see something was still wrong. Benny tried to say with excitement, "Hey! I heard you guys crushed the Bobcats!"

Donny just said, "Yep."

Benny then, once again trying to sound excited, said, "We won too! We beat the Spartans in a close game."

Donny said quietly, "Nice job."

Benny then asked Donny, "Do you want to go out and shoot hoops or play a video game?"

To Benny's surprise, Donny said, "Yeah, let's go downstairs and play a video game."

When they walked downstairs, Benny could tell that Donny's mom looked sad. As they were playing the video game, Benny could not help but break the constant silence. He asked Donny, "Donny, is there something I did or said that you are upset about?"

Donny said, avoiding his question, "I'm glad you are here. Let's just try to have fun."

Benny then said, "How can we have fun if you won't talk with me?"

Donny, looking frustrated, stood up and shut the video game off. He then said, "Let's go see Skipper and play with him."

Benny said, "Okay, let's try and have fun with Skipper."

The boys went outside and played ball with Skipper.

When they finished playing with Skipper, Donny said to Benny, "Someday, I will explain what is going on with me, but, right now, I need some time."

Donny walked away, and Benny rode his bike home.

* * * * *

The semifinals of the play-offs for the Sabreville Basketball League are over. Everyone in the community is surprised that the Gladiators made it to the championship game. They will play the undefeated Knights.

* * * * *

While Benny and his teammates were playing a pickup game at Sabreville Park, Donny came by on his bike with Skipper. Donny walked up to his friends, Petey, Leon, Lamont, Carson, and Anderson, stood next to Benny, and said, "Good job making it to the championship game, guys. I'm happy you made it this far."

Benny was about to say something, but Petey walked up to Donny and asked him, "What is that supposed to mean?"

Donny backed up a bit and explained, "You guys are doing awesome to be in the championship game."

Petey then asked, "You don't think we stand a chance of beating you and your Knights, do you?"

Donny replied, "Hey, listen, I came here to wish you guys luck—"

Before Donny could finish, the Knights basketball team was walking by the courts, and Tony, one of the players for their team, yelled out, "Hey, boys, keep practicing; you're going to need it!"

The Knights basketball team laughed, and then Kyle, another one of their players, started to walk over and say something.

But before he could, Benny, Carson, Anderson, and Petey started toward the Knights, and Carson said, "Let's play a game right now. No referees or coaches, just us against you."

Benny then tried to say something, but Kyle interrupted and said, "Okay, let's do this."

Donny said, "Guys, this is not a good idea. If we argue and someone gets hurt, it will not be worth it."

Tommy, another one of their friends, who was also there with the Knights, agreed with Donny that it was not a good idea.

Tony then walked over to Donny and said with a smirk on his face, "It's okay, Donny. We can beat these chumps without you." Looking at Tommy, he continued, "You can stay; we need at least five to play."

Tommy sighed and said reluctantly, "Okay."

To the surprise of Benny and his friends, Donny got on his bike and rode away with Skipper.

The two teams decided to play a pickup game with the Knights short a player. To no one's surprise, the Knights still won by a wide margin.

Donny ended up watching the game, but from a distance so that he would not be seen. Skipper was also there, lying down next to Donny's bike.

When the game was over, the Knights basketball team continued to trash-talk the Gladiators. The two teams began to push each other and looked as if they were going to start fighting.

When Donny noticed this might happen, he and Scooter quickly rode back towards the basketball courts. As he got close, Donny yelled, "Stop, guys! Just break it up, and everyone go home!"

Kyle walked up to Donny and said, "We don't need you getting hurt before our championship win, Donny. Just go home, and we will see you Saturday for the game."

Donny turned to Benny and said, "Benny, take the guys, and go home."

Benny looked at Donny with disappointment and said to his team, "Okay, guys, let's leave and go home." Before Benny left, he stopped to give Skipper a hug.

Then, Kyle laughed and said, "Ahh, look at that, how cute."

Benny glared at him and was about to say something, but decided not to and turned to walk away.

As Benny began to leave, Kyle grabbed the basketball from Petey.

Petey said, "Hey!"

But before Petey could get the ball back, Kyle started to call out to Skipper, "Skipper, come here, Skipper."

Now, Skipper loved to play ball, and as Kyle put the basketball out in front of him for Skipper to see it, Skipper started to jump up and touch the ball.

As Kyle proceeded to throw the basketball towards the road, he yelled, "Go get it, Skipper! Skipper, go get it!"

Skipper ran for the ball.

Before Benny or Donny could say a word, all that was heard was—

Screech!

Yelp!

A car hit Skipper!

The Knights basketball team, except for Tommy, seeing what happened, ran away and left the scene.

Benny and Donny both yelled out, "No! Skipper! Skipper!" They and the rest of the Gladiators basketball team ran to Skipper, now whimpering in pain.

Benny said, "Oh no, no, no, no, Skipper, no…"

Donny and Benny knelt down to their dog, both in shock and in tears. The two brothers, Carson and Anderson, ran to go get help. Petey and Tommy stood by, not able to say a word and in tears, crying for Skipper.

Benny and Donny, still sobbing gently, carefully picked up their severely hurt dog. As they stood up with Skipper, the boys could hear an ambulance horn. And in the distance, they could see the flashing lights.

Donny quietly whispered in Skipper's ear, "It will be okay, boy. It will be okay."

Benny could not say a word because he was sobbing a bit harder now and trying to control his tears.

Once the ambulance got to the scene, the medical team took the dog, and the boys got in with him. When they arrived at the veterinarian's office, they could see Dr. Holmes running out to greet them. She quickly took the dog out of sight, and both Benny and Donny walked in, still crying and wiping their constant flows of tears.

The boys sat in the vet's office for what seemed like forever.

Finally, Dr. Holmes came out and said to them, "Skipper is resting, and we need to observe him overnight. I also called Mr. Holiday and told him what happened. He said to tell you to pray for Skipper and give him a kiss and a hug for him. He also told me to tell you that he wasn't going to come here because he knew that Skipper had enough love from the both of you to get him through this, and whatever happens, know that there are no hard feelings."

The boys could hardly raise their heads to look at Dr. Holmes. Still sobbing, both boys stood up and walked out. They paused for a moment, looked at each other as if to say something, but still crying uncontrollably, went their separate ways, and walked home.

Chapter V

The Championship Game

It is the next day, the day of the big Sabreville basketball championship game. It seems as if everyone from both sides of town were at the game. All of the parents, grandparents, and community pack inside the gym. The entire Sabreville Elementary student body also fills the gym. The atmosphere is charged with excitement, anticipation, and tension.

You can tell as the Gladiators are warming up that they seem very nervous. On the other side of the court, the Knights look arrogant, cocky, and relaxed.

* * * * *

During the pregame warm-up, Donny and Benny met at half-court. They both wondered if anyone had heard anything about Skipper. The rest of Benny's team, the Gladiators, which consisted of Petey, Lamont, Leon, and the brothers, Carson and Anderson, also came to half-court to find out if Skipper would be okay.

As the boys were meeting at half-court, some of the Knights basketball team came over and interrupted. Kyle said, "Donny, let's go! Don't worry about your precious dog. Let's annihilate these guys."

Donny, red in the face, said back to Kyle, "Back off; this is none of your business!"

The Knights' basketball team all made an "oooooo" noise, and Kyle said back to Donny, "You and your so-called friends can cry about your dog later."

Then, the horn sounded. Time to start the game.

As both teams lined up for the jump ball, right away the Knights had smiles on their faces, and they began to talk trash. Kyle said, "Why bother trying, boys. The same thing will happen, like at the park. We will destroy you." He continued, this time looking at Benny, "I am going to take you to school today, boy."

Right away, the Knights won the jump ball, and for no reason, Jake, a player on the Knights, just ran straight at Benny and lowered his shoulder. Benny landed flat on his back after he was hit.

Of course, a foul was called.

All Benny could think about was, Will this happen to me all game long?

However, Donny saw it happen and immediately ran up to Jake, saying, "Knock it off! Play ball, or I will walk off this court!"

Once again, Benny knew he could count on Donny to stand up for him and protect him.

Donny had always looked out for his best friend, Benny, no matter what.

When the first quarter ended, the score was close, 10 to 8. Benny had zero points for the Gladiators. Heck, he had not even gotten off a shot. Donny for the Knights, however, had scored eight of the Knights' ten points.

* * * * *

Late into the second half, things began to get chippy. The game became more physical, and the Knights were continuing their trash talk. Even though the Knights were the more talented team, they became frustrated because the score was tied, 22 to 22. To add to the Knights' frustration, they were getting into early-foul trouble.

On the other hand, the Gladiators were playing really well as a team. Not as talented as the Knights, but they were playing hard and disciplined.

However, Donny was having the game of his life for the Knights. He had scored now seventeen of the Knights' twenty-two points.

As for Benny, still not one basket.

* * * * *

It was now halftime, and the score was still tied, 22 to 22. As both teams were running to their locker rooms to listen to their coaches, Tony and Kyle of the Knights once again lowered their shoulders into Benny, as if to intimidate him.

As before, Donny noticed this and ran over to Benny to see if he was okay.

Benny said, "I'm okay, Donny."

Donny then said, "You guys are playing a heck of a game; keep it goin'."

Benny told Donny, "You are playing awesome!"

Both boys parted and ran to their respective locker rooms. As Donny walked into the Knights' locker room, he called over Coach Jordan and asked if he could speak to him privately. Donny wanted to tell Coach Jordan that the trash talking and unnecessary fouls needed to stop.

However, Coach Jordan said, "I have to address the entire team, Donny. I do not have time for just you right now."

Donny felt his face turn red with embarrassment at first, and then it began to be a face of anger.

* * * * *

As both teams came out of the locker rooms for the second half, the Gladiators looked pumped up, but the Knights appeared to be a team divided. Donny, who was having the game of his life, just walked out to the court, not excited at all about playing the second half.

As the third quarter went on, the Knights began to pull away. Midway, they were up, 35 to 22. The Gladiators had yet to score in the third quarter. Coach Olander called a time-out.

As the boys were getting back on the court, Jimmy, one of the Knights' players, yelled over to Benny, "Hey, Benny, score any points yet!?"

With a look of embarrassment, Benny could only put his head down and his hands on his knees.

Donny witnessed all this, walked over to Jimmy, and said with a loud tone in his voice, "Enough! Leave Benny alone!"

Again noticing his best friend, Donny, standing up for him, Benny looked at Donny and gave him a nod of appreciation and thanks.

The third quarter continued, and the Gladiators still struggled. At the end of the third quarter, the Knights were ahead, 45 to 30.

During the break between quarters, Carson of the Gladiators called the team over to huddle up so he could give them a pep talk. He was doing everything he could to get the team fired up again.

Then, his brother, Anderson, with his sense of humor and trying to be funny, said, "Hey, guys, if we do not want to win this for ourselves, let's try to win this for the hot girls from school sitting in the stands, watching."

The boys all laughed.

Anderson continued, "We win this champion-ship, we will for sure have dates for the Valentine's Day dance."

Once again, the boys started to laugh.

After Carson's pep talk and Anderson's funny comments, the Gladiators high-fived each other and were ready to go out and play the fourth quarter.

* * * * *

Midway through the fourth quarter, the Gladia-tors begin their comeback. With three minutes to go, they are only down 50 to 43. Benny starts to score as well. He hits two midrange shots and a couple of free throws to help in the rally.

Time on the clock is winding down. There are ten seconds to go, and the game is tied, 53 to 53! The Knights have the ball and call a time-out.

The crowd's buzzing grows louder and louder. The majority of the student body are chanting and cheering for the Knights. As we already know, the Knights are the more popular kids at school.

Both teams are in a huddle, getting instructions from their coaches.

The whistle blows and horn sounds. Immediately, the atmosphere raises to a fever pitch of excitement and tension.

The teams retake the court. The Knights have the ball on the sideline near half-court and are ready to inbound the ball. Tony throws it for the Knights, but the ball is stolen by Benny!

Benny, still having a great fourth quarter, goes in for what appears to be the game-winning lay-up, but out of nowhere, Donny comes over and blocks the ball!

The ball glances off the backboard into Donny's hands!

Five seconds on the clock...

Donny dribbles and races as fast as he can to get a shot off.

Four seconds...three...two...

Donny pulls up inside the top of the key, from twelve feet away—

Out of nowhere, this time it's Benny challenging Donny's shot, but—

Bang!

The whistle blows; the horn sounds.

Donny's shot hits the backboard…rolls around the rim…and misses!!!

Referee has his hand up—no time on the clock—and yells out, "Foul, number twenty-eight!" Benny hit Donny on the arm.

No time left on the clock! Game still tied, 53 to 53!

Donny—the best player on the Knights' team and the one who scored twenty-eight of their fifty-three points—is going to the foul line to shoot free throws.

Benny walks off the court with the rest of his Gladiator teammates. He sits, head down, hands on his knees.

The Knights go to their bench. There's no one on the court but Donny, standing at the foul line.

The crowd is loud now. The student body is chanting, "Donny! Donny! Donny!"

Donny, a very confident kid and the best player on the court, gets the ball from the official who approaches him.

Donny dribbles three times. Bends his knees.

Lets it fly…

Boink!

…and hits the front rim.

Donny misses the first shot!

The crowd lets out a big gasp!

The Knights, hands on their hips, stand courtside.

The tension is rising throughout the gymnasium. The Donny chant continues.

With mixed feelings, Benny is watching his best friend shoot free throws.

Donny steps up to the foul line again and gets the ball from the official.

He does his pre-throw routine again...

He shoots and...

Boink! Boink!

The ball rattles in...and out...and misses again!

The score stays tied, 53 to 53. The game goes into overtime!

The crowd is silent, shocked in disbelief!

Donny, now with his head down, walks over to his team. They all stare at him, still with their hands on their hips, shocked and disappointed.

The Gladiators, happy that they have another chance to win this game, are cheering and excited. Well, at least most of them are, all except for Benny. Benny really does not know how to feel.

On the Knights' side of the court, Coach Jordan says to Donny, "You are going to sit out for this overtime."

Donny, shocked and surprised, takes a seat on the bench. He looks up in the stands to see his mother sitting alone and giving him a thumbs-up, a sign that things are okay. His dad, with his head in his hands, is sitting several seats down from her.

The horn sounds, whistles blow, and the three-minute overtime is about to begin. It starts out with the Knights scoring three baskets in the first minute to go up by six points.

Then, Carson and Anderson, the two brothers, both hit a three-point shot to tie the game with one minute to go.

Score is 59 to 59.

No one scores in the next forty-five seconds.

Fifteen seconds to go.

The crowd is yelling, going wild. Pandemonium is everywhere.

Gladiators now have the ball. Lamont inbounds the ball to Petey. Petey passes to Leon, who then passes the ball to Benny in the corner for a three-point shot. Benny fakes his shot, takes two dribbles, and pulls up for a shot and—

Bang!

Kyle, a Knights player, hits him on the arm.

The referee blows his whistle.

Benny looks up at the clock—only three seconds to go in the game!

Crowd is still going crazy.

Kyle is called for his fifth foul! He has fouled out of the game!

Coach Jordan looks down the bench for a sub and calls out Donny's name for him to go into the game. A couple of the Knights' players, Tony and Jimmy, bump into Benny on purpose before he gets to the foul line to shoot his free throws.

Trembling, Benny is now standing at the foul line, thinking that if he makes these free throws, his Gladiators team will win the league championship. Nervous, breathing heavy, feeling the tension, Benny takes his first shot and…

Swish!

He makes the first shot!

The Gladiators are jumping up and down, barely able to contain and control themselves.

Benny once again takes the ball from the ref. He shoots his second shot and…

Swish!

He makes them both!

The Gladiators are now ahead, 61 to 59. They are hugging and celebrating as if they have won the game!

Then, Coach Jordan calls a time-out with three seconds on the clock. The Knights have to inbound the ball from their own end of the court. Coach Jordan draws up the play.

The horn and referees' whistles blow for the players to come back out on court.

Tommy is to inbound the ball. The referee hands it to him.

Tommy sees Donny standing at half-court with his hands high in the air. Tommy throws it to him like a Hail Mary pass you would see in football.

Donny jumps up above the rest of the Gladiators to catch the ball.

The clock starts…

Two…

Donny pivots.

One second left on the clock…

Donny just heaves the basketball towards the hoop from half-court.

The crowd's cheering is loud!

Once the ball leaves Donny's hand with one second on the clock, everyone in the gymnasium stands up to see the shot.

The horn goes off, and the ball is still soaring through the air towards the basket. Then, you hear...

BOOM!

The ball hits the backboard...bounces a couple of times on the rim...rolls around the rim...

Then, all of a sudden, the ball literally stops for a moment on the rim.

Everyone in the gym is standing, holding their breath, and watching in amazement as the ball sits there for a moment in time and then...

It falls in!

The Knights win, 62 to 61!

The crowd is yelling! High-fiving each other and hugging.

The Knights storm the court and tackle Donny! They hoist Donny up onto their shoulders and parade around the gym.

The Gladiators, just frozen, are standing in amazement, shocked at what they just saw. They are now watching as Donny is being paraded around the gym, and then eventually off the court and into the locker room.

The crowd, which consists of the Sabreville community, parents, and student body, remain in the gymnasium, talking about what a great game they just witnessed.

* * * * *

Donny and Benny eventually met each other at half-court to shake hands and say to each other, "Great game." As they were shaking hands and talking, Benny's parents came to half-court, where the boys were still standing.

Their faces looked sad and upset. Benny's mom spoke up and said softly, "Skipper passed away."

Donny and Benny looked at each other in disbelief and then both teared up, sad about their dog. Benny said, "Where is he?"

Benny's dad said, "He is with Dr. Holmes at the vet office."

Donny then asked with a weeping voice, "Does Mr. Holiday know?"

Benny's dad said, "No. I think you boys should go tell him."

Donny and Benny looked at each, now both sobbing uncontrollably. Donny then said, "Let's go get the guys and let them know."

Benny nodded, unable to talk.

After Donny and Benny told Tommy, Petey, Carson, Anderson, Lamont, and Leon what happened to Skipper, Donny and Benny decided to ride their bikes to the vet's office, pick up Skipper, and take him to Mr. Holiday.

Once both boys arrived at the vet's office, Dr. Mary Holmes met the boys in the lounge. She had Skipper all wrapped up in a blanket covering his wounds. She told the boys she was sorry for their loss and she knew that they had taken care of him and loved him.

Donny and Benny both teared up and took turns holding, kissing, and hugging their dog.

Mary then handed the boys a box to put Skipper in so they could ride their bikes with him over to Mr. Holiday's house.

* * * * *

When the boys arrived at Mr. Holiday's house, he was sitting outside in his rocking chair. The boys, once again tearing up, got off their bikes and walked up to the porch. They still had Skipper wrapped comfortably in the blanket. Donny and Benny, crying now, unable to say a word, looked at Mr. Holiday sitting in his rocking chair and handed Skipper over to him.

Mr. Holiday knew as they handed him the dog and started crying that Skipper had passed away. Mr. Holiday took the dog, held him close, and kissed Skipper on the head. He then said to the boys, "Boys, take a seat and have some lemonade."

The boys sat down, wiping their tears. They both then said at the same time, "We are sorry." They could barely get the words out.

Mr. Holiday replied, "Boys, that is a part of life. Things happen. Sometimes, all we can do is remember the good times and move on."

Both boys just sat there, sad and quiet. Not able to say a word. Finally, Donny said, "Mr. Holiday, if there is anything we can do for you, let us know."

Benny felt so proud of Donny at that moment and thought to himself, Once again, Donny is caring and looking out for others.

Mr. Holiday answered, "Donny, you and Benny are fine young men." He thought for a moment and then said, "There is one thing I would like from both of you."

The boys perked up to listen to what Mr. Holiday had to say.

He continued, "Just make sure you come and visit me every so often."

Benny said, "We sure will, Mr. Holiday."

Both boys stood up walked over to Mr. Holiday to shake his hand.

As they did, Mr. Holiday said, "One more thing I need you boys to do for me. Take Skipper and give him a proper burial. I do not need to be there. This is my good-bye to Skipper. You boys go have a ceremony and bury him where you feel is best."

Both Benny and Donny looked at Mr. Holiday, started to tear up again, not able to talk. They could only nod in agreement. Taking the dog and waving good-bye to Mr. Holiday, they rode away on their bikes.

Chapter VI

A Town Divided Becomes United

The next day, Donny and Benny called their friends, Tommy, Petey, Lamont, Leon, Carson, and Anderson and told them to meet at the railroad tracks that went through the middle of town. Donny and Benny had gotten there early that morning with Skipper and already had a burial site picked out. They had a hole dug right where the crossroads of the town met. Right in the middle.

When the other boys arrived, Leon asked, "Why did you guys pick this spot to bury Skipper?"

Donny answered and said, "Because this is where the middle of town is, and, just maybe, Skipper's burial can be a symbol of hope that our town can come together and not be divided."

Once again, Benny looked at his best friend, Donny, as proud as ever. Benny then said, "There is a reason this happened to Skipper. We need to have hope."

The boys showed that they understood what Donny and Benny were saying by nodding and then coming together as Benny and Donny placed Skipper in the hole they'd dug. Once Donny and Benny finished shoveling the dirt over Skipper, who was still in his blanket, all of the boys joined hands and knelt down in honor of Skipper.

The night before, Donny and Benny had written something for Skipper's burial ceremony. They each read what they'd written and took turns talking about Skipper. Then, the boys agreed to keep holding hands and have moments of silence and prayer. After a while, Benny and

Donny's friends, one by one, came over to give them each a hug and say good-bye and that they would see them tomorrow.

Once everyone left, as Benny gave Donny a hug, Donny said, "Wait, Benny, don't leave yet. I have something to tell you."

Benny said, "Okay."

Donny sat there for a minute; tears began running down his face.

Benny asked, "What's wrong, Donny?"

Donny said with a cracking voice, "I have been quiet these days and distant for a reason, and I want to explain." Still with a quavering voice, Donny continued, "My mom and dad are getting a divorce."

Benny did not say a word. He was speechless.

Donny, pretty much crying now, was not done yet. He then said, "That's not all of it." Barely able to talk, Donny went on, "My mom is sick with cancer."

Benny did not know what to say. He again was speechless as he knew his face was growing sad and pale. Motionless, he sat there looking at Donny as Donny wept.

Benny was silent, thinking to himself, Donny is someone I thought had it all. Great character, rich family, popular in school, basketball star, and hero. Now this. How can this happen to the town hero? He has it all. However, does he really?

Then, Benny said, "Donny, just like you have been for me and for everyone else you know, I will be there for you."

Donny abruptly got up, gave Benny one last hug, and got on his bike.

It began to rain.

* * * * *

Donny is racing home, tears blinding him as he is riding his bike in the pouring rain. As he comes to an intersection, he races through and then—

Screeeech!

Bang!

A car hits Donny.

The car launches Donny off his bike, into the air. Donny then finally lands on the curb on the other side of the road. His body is contorted. Blood is coming out of his nose and mouth.

People get out of their cars and call 9-1-1. In a matter of minutes, all you can hear are the sirens of the ambulance and police cars. Donny is safely but quickly placed on a stretcher. He is unconscious, barely breathing, and in critical condition. He is placed into the ambulance and rushed to the hospital.

It did not take long for the news to get out to the Sabreville community. Everyone from both sides of town gather in the hospital waiting area. People from both sides of town are sitting or standing, talking together, praying together for Donny to be okay. Benny and Donny's parents sit with each other and hold hands in silence. Some of the Knights' players, Kyle, Tony, Jimmy, and Jake, are in the waiting room with the rest of the community, looking sad and worried for their friend.

Benny and the rest of his friends cannot sit still; they are pacing. Benny so desperately wants to see Donny and know how he is doing.

The doctor finally comes out of Donny's room. He goes over to Donny's parents and says, "Come with me, folks."

Everyone is sitting, holding hands with at least one other person. Several people are crying, wiping their tears with tissues. Everyone is anticipating the news on how Donny is doing.

Benny walks over to try to hear what the doctor is saying to Donny's parents, but cannot hear them talking. He is worried and concerned for his friend. Then, he sees Donny's parents' reaction after the doctor tells them Donny's condition. Donny's mom is crying in his dad's chest.

Benny's heart is pounding. He thinks the worst. Then, Donny's parents walk by Benny to go into Donny's room. The doctor walks in with them. They are in Donny's room for what feels like hours.

The waiting is excruciating and painful for Benny. As Benny is sitting with the rest of his friends, Carson has his arm around him to comfort him.

Benny then sees Mr. Holiday, with his cane, limping towards him. Mr. Holiday says, while specifically looking at Benny, "Boys, your friend will need you more than ever. The support you give him will get him through this." He sticks his hand out and shakes each of the boys' hands.

Then, Donny's parents and the doctor walk out of Donny's hospital room. Benny is crying with his face in his hands. Donny's mom comes over to Benny and says, "Benny, I am sure Donny would love for you to go in there and be by his side."

Benny stands up, and Donny's mom gives him a hug. Benny, barely able to gather himself and calm down, walks into Donny's hospital room. He sits next to Donny's hospital bed, takes Donny's hand, and begins to cry more and more. He then looks closely at Donny.

Donny is lying there with his eyes closed. He has all kinds of bandages on his face, arms, and legs. Tubes are running through his arms and nose.

Benny, still weeping, finally says, "Donny, I will be here for you, because you have always been here for me." He continues with his voice cracking, heart in his throat, "I will be by your side, no matter what."

The End

About the Author

I am currently a college business professor. I teach sport management, research, marketing, and leadership courses. In 2011, I achieved my doctorate in leadership studies. I have been teaching at the college level for sixteen years, since 2005. I have also coached for twenty-four years. I have coached high school volleyball, tennis, baseball, and basketball. I was named All-County All-Star Volleyball Coach in 2013 and 2014. I also had the opportunity to be a head junior college volleyball and basketball coach.

I was born in Buffalo, New York, and raised in Cheektowaga, New York. I now live in Shelby, Ohio. I have two sons, Carson and Anderson Brubaker. Carson is sixteen-years-old, and Anderson is fourteen. My mom and dad, Irene and Ken Brubaker Sr., still live in Cheektowaga, New York. I have two older sisters, Debbi Socha and Joy Ostrander. They've given me three nieces, Anna, Grace, and Kelsea, and two nephews, Tom and Peter. I love when my sons can get together with their cousins. We have the best times getting together with family.

My contact information is:
kbrubaker1280@gmail.com

CPSIA information can be obtained
at www.ICGtesting.com
Printed in the USA
BVHW090039280421
605944BV00007B/1726